MAKING
THE TEAM

THE
CHALLENGE

Written by Alan Durant
Illustrated by Maggie Roman

Thanks to Inclusive Minds (the CIC supporting and championing inclusion and diversity in children's books) for introducing us to Kay and Gabriella through their network of Inclusion Ambassadors.

Special thanks also to Harrison, Parker and Reegan.

Titles in the Making the Team Series:

The Challenge

The Battle

Up and Running

Paying the Penalty

Taking a Stand

The Final

Badger Publishing Limited
Oldmedow Road,
Hardwick Industrial Estate,
King's Lynn PE30 4JJ

Telephone: **01553 816 082**
www.badgerlearning.co.uk

2 4 6 8 10 9 7 5 3

The Challenge
ISBN 978-1-78837-655-6

Commissioning Editor: Sarah Rudd
Editor: Claire Morgan
Designer: Bigtop Design
Cover: alphaspirit.it/Shutterstock

THE CHALLENGE

Contents

Characters

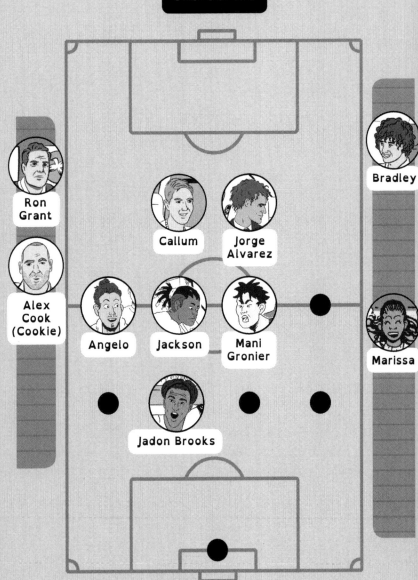

Ron Grant

Alex Cook (Cookie)

Callum

Jorge Alvarez

Angelo

Jackson

Mani Gronier

Bradley

Marissa

Jadon Brooks

backheel: a pass or shot made using the heel of the foot

box-to-box: a midfielder who is equally good at both attacking and defending

dyslexia: a learning difficulty that makes reading harder, but does not affect intelligence

far post: the goalpost that is farthest away from the ball when it is kicked towards the goal

near post: the goalpost nearest to the ball when it is kicked at the goal

one-twos: a quick pass made between two players to get past a defender

physio: someone who is qualified to treat injuries through massage, exercise or heat therapy

stamina: the ability to keep up physical or mental effort for a long time

CHAPTER ONE

BE BOLD.

Callum Cooper stared at the two words on the wall behind manager Ron Grant's desk. He had never been in this office before and he didn't feel bold. He felt scared.

Callum looked at the row of clocks on the shelf by the window. Time was ticking away. Was this the moment that his football career at Premier League Stanford FC would come to an end? But, hold on, Jackson was here. Angelo, Yuri and Rav too. They were all top players. The Under-21 team coach Jason Smith was in the room as well, and he was smiling. So maybe it wasn't bad news...

Grant coughed.

"Now, lads," he began, "you're probably wondering why I asked you to come today."

The five teenage footballers stayed silent. Callum could hardly bear the tension.

"Well, I have a challenge for you," Grant stated.

A challenge? Callum breathed a small sigh of relief. He wasn't getting the push.

"Jason here," Grant continued, nodding at the Under-21 coach, "tells me that you young men can play a bit — and I don't mean FIFA on your Xbox."

The teenagers laughed nervously. What was this all about?

Grant sat up a little in his chair.

"Stanford is a club that has a tradition of putting faith in young players," he said. "We like to encourage young talent and, let's face it, we don't have the money that some of our rivals have. We need to invest in youth. We're very proud of our academy. We think it's one of the top training programmes in the country."

Grant paused and his eyes narrowed. "This is your chance to prove yourselves."

Callum felt a shiver in his chest. He knew Ron Grant's reputation. His players liked him, but step out of line and he'd be down on you like a tonne of bricks. He was tough.

"I'm giving you five lads the chance to train with the First Team for a week," said Grant. "Impress me and you'll be part of the squad for our pre-season tournament."

Grant's words were met with more silence. Callum could sense that the others were in shock, just like him.

"Well, are you happy? You don't seem it!" Grant grunted.

"We're happy, boss," said Jackson, who was the Under-21 captain. "Aren't we, boys?"

There was a mumble of agreement.

The manager waved his hand. "Right then, off you go," he smiled, "You've got training to get to and I've got contracts to sign."

CHAPTER TWO

Training was harder than Callum was used to. It was definitely a step up from the Under-21s. Lots of steps in fact.

The drills were faster and sharper. Your control had to be spot on and your reactions almost instant.

Callum's control wasn't good enough in the two-touch exercises. The ball was passed around and across a circle of four players, trying to keep it away from the one in the middle.

Callum ended up in the middle more than anyone else. He saw a couple of the senior players shake their heads as the ball bounced away off his foot again.

The attack vs defence drill didn't go any better.

Callum was a striker. There were three attackers against two defenders, but Callum barely managed a shot.

The two defenders were both full internationals — one was club captain Jadon Brooks — and they were impossible to get past.

"You're not using your heads, lads," said Alex Cook, the First Team coach. "Think about it."

Callum watched Brooks closely. He began to notice where the defender was leaving space for an attack. Callum knew that he needed to take advantage of this. He needed to advance closer to the edge of the box.

After that, the attackers did manage to make one clear chance, but Callum hit his shot straight at the keeper who made an easy save.

Lunch was in the club cafe.

Callum was so hungry. He loved burgers and pizza, but there was only healthy food on the menu — lots of veg and salad.

The players had strict diets to help improve their energy and stamina. But the food was tasty, and there was plenty of it, so Callum was happy.

He sat on a table with the other young players from the manager's office — Jackson, Angelo, Rav and Yuri. They talked about the morning's training. Everyone agreed it was very hard.

The challenge that Grant had set of training with the First Team was testing them to the max. Callum hoped he had enough talent to be chosen to play in the pre-season tournament.

After lunch, the young players had to do some tests. The physio watched, took readings and made notes on his iPad.

Then there was a gym session.

Callum loved playing football, but he hated the gym. It was such hard work. Sit-ups, squats, bench presses, lifting weights...

Callum was puffing before he even got on the treadmill to jog and sprint.

The physio shook his head. "We need to get your fitness levels up, son," he said.

Callum was too breathless to say anything.

Jackson came over and handed Callum a bottle of water.

"Tough, isn't it?" Jackson said with a smile.

Jackson didn't look like he'd found the gym tough. He looked as fresh as when he'd started.

Callum would have to work harder if he wanted to make the First Team.

CHAPTER THREE

Callum's best friend was called Bradley. They met at primary school and had been mates ever since.

That evening, Callum went to Bradley's house. Bradley's room was on the ground floor because he used a wheelchair full time.

Bradley was Stanford FC's biggest fan and went to every match. Everyone at the club knew him. His room was full of signed player pictures, club scarves and shirts.

Bradley was thrilled when Callum told him about the challenge to try and make the First Team. Now he wanted to know everything about Callum's day.

He laughed about all the clocks in the manager's office.

"Ron Grant is obsessed with time," said Bradley. "Didn't you know?"

Callum shook his head.

"He fines players if they're even one minute late for training," Bradley continued. "You need to make sure you're always on time."

"Don't worry, I will," said Callum. "I don't want to get on the wrong side of Grant. I really want to make the First Team squad for the tournament next week."

"Yeah, that would be so cool," Bradley nodded.

The tournament was an international one with eight teams from different countries. Some of the top teams in Europe were taking part. There would be two groups of four with the winners of each group playing in the final.

Callum would love to get into the Stanford squad for a chance to show off his skills, but he wasn't feeling very hopeful.

"The First Team players are so good, Bradley," he sighed.

"So are you, Callum. Think of all those goals you scored for the Under-21s," said Bradley.

Callum frowned. "But the First Team is another level," he moaned.

Callum told Bradley about the attack vs defence drill and how good the defenders were.

Bradley smiled at his friend. "You've just got to believe, Callum. I know you can do it."

Callum nodded. Bradley was right. He always had a way of making things seem possible.

"You don't want to give up like your dad," added Bradley.

"No, I don't," Callum agreed quietly.

Callum hadn't seen his dad since he left home a year ago.

He used to be a talented footballer when he was Callum's age, but a couple of bad injuries had ended his career almost before it began. He never got over it, and made his family's life miserable.

Callum wasn't sorry when he left. He just hoped that wherever his dad was, he wasn't making anyone else unhappy.

"Now, how about a game of FIFA?" Bradley suggested with a grin. "I'll show you some great moves that you can use in training tomorrow."

Callum laughed. "Come on then," he said. "But you know I'll beat you."

"In your dreams," Bradley replied.

CHAPTER FOUR

Ever since Callum had started at Stanford Academy, aged nine, all he wanted was to be a footballer.

He struggled at school. He wasn't good at reading or writing or maths. Tests showed he had dyslexia, but more than that, he just didn't like school. The only thing Callum really did like was PE lessons — football most of all.

The club insisted on young players continuing with their education after leaving school. Callum was at college doing a BTEC course. It was about sport, but he couldn't see the point. He was going to be a footballer. It was really hard finding time to study with all the training and the exercises he'd been given to practise at home. And, of course, the matches. Callum lived for the matches.

It wasn't easy at the academy. Everyone there wanted to make it as a professional footballer, but only a few would. Callum's mum told him once that only one of every thousand baby seahorses survived. The odds were about the same for young footballers making it to a professional level.

So far, Callum had been lucky, but he expected every academy year to be his last. There were other players who seemed so much more talented than him. But somehow, they were let go and he was kept on. He had a lucky habit of scoring goals. He could do nothing for a whole game and then pop up at the end and score the winning goal. That was his skill.

Callum was the top scorer for the Under-21s, but training with the First Team was a whole new ball game. Still, this was his chance to shine. He had to take it.

The day before had shown Callum that he needed to up his game. He needed to be more like the other players from the Under-21 team, especially Jackson.

Jackson never stopped. You couldn't take your eyes off him. Angelo was a great dribbler, Rav was a top passer, Yuri was quick and strong, but Jackson was the heartbeat of the team. He ran, he tackled, he won the ball and used it. He was a box-to-box player. Callum was never going to be like that. But he could try.

Callum made sure he arrived at the club early. It wasn't just because of what Bradley said about the manager and time, but also because he wanted to do half an hour in the gym before training began. He was tall, but his body wasn't as powerful as most of his teammates. As a striker, he needed more upper body strength.

Callum started with some barbell squats — front and back — and then moved on to do bench presses. He was coming to an end when the physio looked in.

"So, you're taking my words seriously," he said with an approving nod. "Good for you. But don't overdo it. You've got a long and hard day ahead."

CHAPTER FIVE

The physio was right. It was a very long and very hard day. So was the next day and the one after that. At the end of each day, Callum ached all over.

Some of the other young players were staying with host families, but Callum only lived five minutes from the club so he was allowed to live at home. Right now, he'd never been happier to be there. When he arrived home tired, his mum ran him a hot bath and then fed him a delicious dinner. By 9.30pm he was in bed and fell asleep instantly. No late-night FIFA games with Bradley!

The long sleeps definitely improved his concentration, but he still felt like a little fish in a big pond.

The first thing he saw when he walked into the club grounds each morning was the players' car park full of Range Rovers, Ferraris and Mercedes-Benzes. Machines from another world. A dreamworld.

Callum tried hard in training, but he just couldn't seem to get his feet to do what he wanted. In the small-sided games that ended each session, he lost the ball often. When the ball came his way, it just wouldn't stick, or a defender would step in and whip it away from him. Jackson, Rav, Yuri and Angelo all seemed to be doing better than Callum. He wasn't even scoring goals! He had taken some shots, but few were on target and none of them went in.

On the third morning, Ron Grant came to training. He hardly ever did that. He normally left it to his coaches. Seeing the boss made Callum more nervous than ever. He tried some fancy footwork, but the ball got caught between his feet and he fell over.

Jadon Brooks laughed. He pulled Callum to his feet, saying, "Keep it simple, mate."

At the end of the day, Callum stomped out into the car park, sure that his dream was over. He was out of his depth and this time his luck had run out.

"Want a lift, kid?" said a voice.

Callum turned to see the burly figure of Jorge Alvarez, Stanford's record goal scorer.

Alvarez was in the last year of his contract before retiring and didn't play much for the First Team any more. But still, he was a club legend, and he was Callum's hero.

"You don't have a car, do you?" Alvarez asked. His Spanish accent was strong even after all the years he'd lived in the UK.

Callum finally managed to find his voice. "I... er... I mean... no. No, I don't have a car."

Alvarez pressed his key fob and his shiny black Mercedes beeped and flashed. "Jump in then. Let's go."

Callum sent a quick text to his mum to let her know he was getting in a car with one of football's biggest legends.

The short drive that followed was the greatest moment of Callum's life.

Alvarez had been watching Callum all week. He'd seen his problems and how hard he was trying. Callum reminded the expert striker of how he was at Callum's age when he was desperate to get into the Valencia First Team.

"Like you, I tried too hard. I tried to use skills I did not yet have," Alvarez said with a shrug and a smile. "You and I, Callum, we have a talent. A talent that makes us special."

Alvarez grinned. "We score goals. Don't change your style. Trust your instincts and you will do very well."

Callum let the words sink in. Alvarez was right. Callum had been feeling so nervous that he was overthinking things. He needed to let his feet do the talking.

As they pulled up outside Callum's house, Alvarez held his hand out and Callum realised he wanted him to shake it. Shake Jorge Alvarez's hand! He couldn't wait to tell Bradley.

When Callum got out of the car, he felt
like his whole world was brighter. What had
seemed impossible was possible again.

CHAPTER SIX

The next day was Callum's best by far. Perhaps the extra time he'd spent in the gym was working? He felt fitter and sharper. Alvarez's words had put a spring in his step. He still made mistakes, but not nearly as many as before. He was doing well.

The key to the improvement was his movement. He never stood still. In the defence vs attack drills, he was on the move all the time. He ran in behind, played quick one-twos, and hung back a little when his strike partner made a move.

The goals started to come. He played the same way in the match as he had at the end of training. He kept captain Jadon Brooks and the other defenders on their toes. He made runs out to the wing, darts into the centre; he went near post, far post, and stayed far back for the ball to come to him.

Three chances came his way and he took them all. The third was a backheel that wrong-footed Brooks and the goalie, sailing into the back of the net. Jackson was the first to congratulate him.

"Awesome skill!" he said, offering Callum his palm in a high five.

Callum was delighted, but then he saw Brooks coming towards him and he started to worry. What if the captain thought he was showing off?

But Brooks smiled and shook his head. "Nice work. Glad to see you didn't follow my advice."

Callum smiled back. The thing was, though, that he had kept it simple. The finish may have looked fancy, but it was the only option. He was just doing what came naturally: trying to score. And this time he'd got it right.

Later that afternoon, when the players were showered, dressed, and ready to leave, the five young players were called to the manager's office again.

As before, the Under-21 coach Jason Smith was there, but looking more serious this time. He nodded at Callum, but didn't smile.

Once more, Callum's eyes went to the row of ticking clocks. His gaze moved over them and then to the right, out of the window. He could see the pitch, looking as perfect as the green cloth on a snooker table. All he wanted was to be out there, playing on it. He'd done well today, but surely that wasn't enough. If only he'd had more time, a few more days...

"So, lads, you took my challenge. Well done for that," Ron Grant began. "Some of you rose to it and some of you didn't. That's the way things are."

He gazed at the players with steely eyes. "Rav and Yuri, you boys have got a lot of ability and I'd really like to keep you on. But I'm afraid I've had to make the difficult decision to let you go. The academy staff will do all they can to find you a new club. Thank you for all your hard work and I wish you the very best in the future. This isn't the end. It's just the end of your time here."

Callum turned to look at his teammates. Rav and Yuri were pale as ghosts. Jason Smith stepped forwards and shook their hands.

"Sort your stuff out, lads, and I'll see you in the lounge," he said quietly.

The two young men turned and shuffled out of the room.

"So, then there were three," Grant continued. "Jackson and Angelo. You've impressed the coaches all week with your attitude, application and skill. You're in the squad for the tournament. Congratulations."

Again, Jason Smith stepped forwards and shook his players' hands. Jackson and Angelo left the room in a very different mood from their teammates.

"And that just leaves you, Callum."

Callum could hardly breathe. Was this the end for him?

Grant's look was not encouraging.

Callum could feel tears in his eyes and fought to keep them back. This was it, then.

"I have to say I wasn't impressed by what I saw of you the other day. But it seems that others were," said Grant. "You have supporters here. And if a Stanford legend and my own First Team captain say you're worth taking a punt on, then who am I to disagree? So, you're in the squad."

Callum released a breath and grinned. But there was more.

Ron raised a wagging finger and sternly said, "But I expect you to work hard. Score."

"I will," Callum promised.

His grin was even wider now.

He'd taken the challenge and, somehow, he'd passed. He'd made the squad.

He was in!

Further activities

1. Ron Grant has a BE BOLD poster in his office. Design an inspirational poster that you think would help young football players when they are feeling nervous.

2. Callum has had an amazing day and made it into the First Team. Write a diary entry from Callum's point of view which describes his day and how he was feeling at different points of the story.

Enjoyed this book?

Follow the Making the Team journey
across all six brilliant stories!